The Trouble with Valentines

Elaine Moore

Illustrated by
Lori Savastano

A
LITTLE
APPLE
PAPERBACK

SCHOLASTIC INC.
New York Toronto London Auckland Sydney

No part of this publication may be reproduced in whole or in part, or stored in a retrieval system, or transmitted in any form or by any means, electronic, mechanical, photocopying, recording, or otherwise, without written permission of the publisher. For information regarding permission, write to Scholastic Inc., Attention: Permissions Department, 555 Broadway, New York, NY 10012.

ISBN 0-590-37234-3

Text copyright © 1998 by Elaine Moore.
Illustrations copyright © 1998 by Scholastic Inc.
All rights reserved. Published by Scholastic Inc.
LITTLE APPLE PAPERBACKS and logo are trademarks of Scholastic Inc.

12 11 10 9 8 7 6 5 4 3 2 1   8 9/9 0 1 2 3/0

Printed in the U.S.A.   40

First Scholastic printing, January 1998

*For Ryan,
my always
and forever
Valentine*

1

Lexi Brinkley sat on the edge of her chair with her elbows propped on the desk in front of her, her head balanced in the palms of her hands. She had been thinking about valentines all morning and all afternoon.

What was the hold-up? she wondered. It was February 4th, for Pete's sake, and a Friday at that! As far as Lexi was concerned, this had been a whole wasted week!

The third grade had learned about calendars way back in September. Everyone got to pick a favorite month. Most of the kids picked December because of Christmas, except for AnnMarie, Lexi's very best friend, who picked December because of Hanukkah. Some kids picked the month that had their birthdays. Others picked October because of Halloween. Not Lexi. She picked February because of Valentine's Day. It was her favorite time of the year. To celebrate, she dotted the "i" in her name with a heart.

Now she sat wondering when their pretty young teacher, Miss Delaney, would talk to the class about the party. It was almost dismissal time and there she was still talking with the new girl, Candace.

It was going to be a terrific party. Lexi's mom was bringing the cupcakes. But there was still so much more to plan. The classroom needed to be decorated, too. Right now the only hearts in the whole room were the ones on the calendar, and those were white with numbers, not red with arrows.

Lexi was staring at the ceiling, imagining what the room would look like with a big dangling heart mobile, when Miss Delaney began printing large block letters on the chalkboard.

MONDAY, FEBRUARY 14

Lexi could hear Harold, who sat beside her and across from AnnMarie, tapping his fingers under his desk. She knew what he was doing. He was trying to figure out how many days they had left.

"Boys and girls," their teacher said. "Valentine's Day is on a Monday this year, so we'll need everything done by next Friday."

As Miss Delaney chattered gaily about Valentine's Day her face lit up, her eyes twinkled, and a pretty dimple showed in her left cheek. Lexi sneaked a quick peek at AnnMarie.

"Please copy this list of supplies in your homework notebook," their teacher went on. "In a few days, I'll give a class list so you can start addressing your valentines."

Lexi raised her hand. "Will Candace's name be on the list?"

Miss Delaney smiled. "Yes, it will. And how nice of you to remind me. We wouldn't want anyone excluded. Valentine's Day is a special day for friendships."

Lexi felt AnnMarie look at her. They lived across the street from each other and had been best friends since forever.

Lexi raised her hand again. Miss Delaney blinked her eyes in surprise. "Lexi, do you have another question?"

Lexi put her finger to her chin. "Yes. When you said 'special,' it made me wonder. Do you have somebody who's your special valentine?"

Miss Delaney blushed. "Oh, my goodness. I have more than one special valentine."

Lexi's eyes grew wide. "You do?"

"Yes. I have twenty-six."

Lexi saw AnnMarie's mouth drop. "Twenty-six?"

Meanwhile, Harold's fingers were tapping like crazy. Candace had turned around in her chair. Her finger was going up and down as she counted the kids in their class. "Twenty-five," she said.

"I'm afraid you left out someone important," Miss Delaney said.

"Who?" Candace asked.

"You!" Miss Delaney laughed. "But weren't you smart to figure out my puzzle."

Lexi shook her head. "That's not what I meant."

"What did you mean then?" Miss Delaney asked.

"I meant a valentine who is your age."

Miss Delaney fanned her face. "Goodness, Lexi. Such questions! All of you should know by now that you are very special in my heart."

Everyone beamed.

But it still wasn't what Lexi needed to know. She raised her hand again. That was when AnnMarie gave her a hard kick under the desk.

Just then the warning bell rang for dismissal. Mrs. Simmons, the school secretary, began calling out the bus numbers over the loudspeaker.

A few minutes later, Lexi and AnnMarie slung their backpacks over their shoulders and charged down the hall. They bumped right into the handsome fifth grade teacher, Mr. Grant.

"Whoa, ladies! You almost swept me off my feet," he said, winking at them.

Lexi couldn't help it. Her face flamed at the very thought of sweeping someone like Mr. Grant off his feet. She had to grab onto AnnMarie to keep from falling herself! And then, like a whirlwind, the thought hit her.

Gosh! Lexi couldn't help but wonder, Did Mr. Grant have a special valentine?

2

"It's not fair," Lexi told AnnMarie, who was staying over Saturday night. "Every grown-up should have a special valentine, especially Miss Delaney. Come on. I want to ask my mom something."

Mrs. Brinkley was a florist, but instead of working in her shop tonight she was making corsage bows at the kitchen table. February was always a busy month for a florist.

Lexi wrapped her arms around her

mother's neck, giving her a hug. "Mom, do you have a special valentine?"

Mrs. Brinkley patted Lexi's arms. "Besides you? Hmmmm. Why don't you ask your father?"

"Daddy!" Lexi hollered downstairs where her father was building birdhouses. "Mom needs to know if she has a special valentine."

Before Lexi and AnnMarie knew what was happening, Mr. Brinkley dashed up the stairs. He swept his wife out of her chair. With both girls watching wide-eyed, they did a silly dance. Then, Mr. Brinkley planted a loud kiss right on his wife's lips.

"Wow!" AnnMarie gasped.

"That's nothing," Lexi said as they escaped to the family room. "You should see them on their anniversary — totally romantic."

"Maybe," AnnMarie mused out loud, "since your father is so good at it, he could be Miss Delaney's valentine."

Lexi gawked at her best friend. "Are you wacko? My father's married to my mother! He can't be the teacher's valentine. Maybe you should volunteer *your* father."

AnnMarie made a face. "No way! I wouldn't want someone who drilled holes in people's mouths for *my* valentine. It's bad enough having a *dentist* for a father."

Lexi threw a piece of popcorn at Ann-Marie. "What if your father was an undertaker? Wouldn't you just die!" she blurted between giggles.

As soon as they heard Mr. Brinkley clomp down the steps, the girls trooped back into the kitchen.

"Seriously, Mom," Lexi said. "When you met Dad, how did you know for sure that you were valentines?"

Mrs. Brinkley put her bows aside for a moment and glanced over her shoulder at the girls. "He sent me flowers with the sweetest note. After all, flowers *are* the language of love."

"Wow." AnnMarie was impressed.

10

"Yeah," Lexi agreed as they returned to the family room to watch television. "If only someone would send Miss Delaney flowers."

Later, when their favorite program came on, Lexi stared at the television without watching. She was still thinking about her teacher. The program paused for a commercial, but she and AnnMarie continued staring at the television anyway.

A lady with dark wavy hair was at a party with a bunch of grown-ups. The room had a fireplace, and the whole time the lady kept glancing at a handsome man in a ski sweater. Soon, the man was carrying two cups of hot chocolate and walking toward the lady. Wow! Love at first sight. But, no! As soon as he got close, she blinked her eyes and sadly turned away. What was the matter? Didn't she like hot chocolate? Then the commercial showed the man opening his medicine cabinet and pulling out a bottle of mouthwash. A few seconds later, the man and lady were kissing in a

11

field of daisies as a spring breeze blew her straw hat up in the air.

Then came the best part, a peppy little jingle, "For the sweetest kisses miles around use Hope mouthwash," followed by the deep voice of an announcer. "Remember, with Hope there's always hope."

Lexi let out a long sigh.

"Huh," AnnMarie said. "My dad's got that stuff."

Lexi blinked. "What stuff?"

"Hope mouthwash. He's got closets full." AnnMarie examined her fingernails. "My mother says that's how we got my brother."

"Wow," they both said at once before dissolving into another batch of giggles. "Powerful stuff."

"Bedtime, girls!" Mrs. Brinkley interrupted from the kitchen. "You have to get your beauty rest. I'll be up in a few minutes."

"If our teacher doesn't have a special

valentine on Valentine's Day, I am going to be so sorry," Lexi said to AnnMarie as they started up the stairs. "I say we can't let it happen."

AnnMarie agreed. "It should be someone like your dad. The way he swept your mother off her feet and danced around the kitchen was so cool. Not to mention the flowers and sweet little note."

Lexi's face lit up with a wide smile. "Of course! Why didn't we think of him before?"

AnnMarie blinked. "But you already said your dad . . ."

"No, silly! Not my dad. Mr. Grant!" Lexi exclaimed.

AnnMarie's mouth dropped open. "What could be more perfect — two teachers!" AnnMarie chattered on. "Besides, everyone says he looks like Superman the way his black hair curls down over his forehead. He is *so* cute."

Lexi clapped her hands. "Yes!"

"And," AnnMarie continued as she

reached into her tote bag for her pajamas, "last week, Monica heard a fifth-grader on her bus say that Mr. Grant isn't married. He doesn't even keep a girlfriend's picture on his desk."

"Great!" Lexi kicked her shoes into the corner and dropped her nightgown over her head. "Let's make up love letters to each of them."

"Like 'I love you, signed Miss Delaney' or 'I want to kiss your lips, signed Mr. Grant.' No, that won't work," AnnMarie giggled. "Teachers are smart. He'll ask her and she'll ask him and we'll get detention."

"Well, what if we don't sign any names?" Lexi climbed up to sit in the middle of her bed. "What if we sign it 'Your secret admirer' like the cards we saw at the mall. We could leave the notes on their desks."

AnnMarie nodded. "Still won't work. When Robert left his homing pigeon report on Miss Delaney's desk instead of putting it in her writing basket, it was three whole days before she found it. Mr. Grant's desk is probably worse. They'd never find our notes."

"Then we'll leave something else," Lexi said, determined.

"Like?"

"Don't rush me. I'm thinking." Suddenly, Lexi snapped her fingers. "What if Mr. Grant gave Miss Delaney flowers?"

"Yeah." The girls fell back on the pillows, giggling. "The language of love."

Still giggling, Lexi rolled over on her stomach. "I'll get some flowers from my mom, and we'll put them on Miss Delaney's desk with a note from her secret admirer."

"Except to make it really good," Ann-Marie said, "we need to give Mr. Grant something, too."

Lexi wrinkled her nose. "No socks."

AnnMarie agreed. Socks were too ordinary. The same with ties. Men always got those and heart underwear was too embarrassing. It had to be something easy. Free was important, too, because they didn't have much money.

"I know!" Lexi shouted. "For the sweetest kisses miles around . . ."

"Perfect! My dad's mouthwash!" AnnMarie exclaimed while hitting Lexi with a pillow.

Whomp!

Quickly, Lexi grabbed the pillow. *Whomp! Whomp!* Bull's-eye!

AnnMarie was still giggling when Lexi put down the pillow and grew quiet. "This is important," she told AnnMarie. "Whatever we do, we can't let Miss Delaney or Mr. Grant find out. That would be awful. The only way this will work is if no one else knows."

"Like a secret club," AnnMarie said.

Lexi beamed. She swatted AnnMarie with a pillow one last time before turning out the light. "The Valentine Club!"

The two Valentines wasted no time. Immediately after church and with her mother's permission, Lexi picked three red roses and two sprigs of fern from her mother's flower case. She hooked a thin red ribbon around the stems and tied it in a tiny bow. All the Valentines needed now was the note from Miss Delaney's secret admirer.

Lexi phoned AnnMarie.

"It's all set," AnnMarie said. "My dad is driving us to school. He has a root canal and has to get to his office early. I told him we had a special project. He's so busy thinking about the root canal, he didn't even ask what."

Lexi couldn't believe their luck. "Do you have the Hope mouthwash?"

"All ready in my backpack," AnnMarie replied.

"Super. Watch out, Miss Delaney!" Lexi whooped with happiness. "What about the notes?"

"I did them on my computer," AnnMarie answered. "The only thing I don't understand is how are we supposed to get this stuff on the teachers' desks without anyone seeing?"

"Easy," Lexi said. "You know how when it's cold, Mrs. Simmons opens the school doors early so the walkers can stay warm in the lobby? Nobody will see us and even if they do, we just smile and act like we didn't know the rules."

"Wow!" AnnMarie raved. "This is going to be so cool."

3

Monday morning was blustery cold with thick gray clouds. On such a dreary day, red roses from a secret admirer would be just what Miss Delaney would want to see.

Lexi held the flowers close, protecting them against the wind as she and Ann-Marie climbed out of Dr. Hampton's car. Just as they hoped, the doors were open and the lobby empty. Moving quickly, the girls started down the hallway with their gifts. Suddenly, they froze as teachers' voices drifted toward them from the library.

AnnMarie grabbed Lexi's sleeve. "Duck!"

They tiptoed past the library door. Shhh! The teachers were having a meeting. Lexi didn't breathe again until they turned the corner and entered their classroom.

AnnMarie sucked in her breath and shuddered. "It's spooky with no one here."

Lexi was too scared to say anything. Working quickly, she put the flowers on their teacher's desk. While she positioned the red bow, AnnMarie unfolded the note and set it beside the flowers.

"Hurry," Lexi urged. "The buses will be here any minute and we still have to give Mr. Grant his mouthwash."

Together, they peeked out the door. Good. The coast was clear. Quickly, they dashed down the hall and into Mr. Grant's room.

"Wow! Fifth grade is so neat!" AnnMarie whispered.

She was staring at a jar labeled SWAMP WATER while Lexi peered at an iguana in a glass aquarium. Neither of the girls had been in Mr. Grant's room before. For a second, they forgot why they'd come. And then the iguana flicked its tongue.

Lexi almost flew out of her skin. "Yi-ikes! L-l-let's get going."

AnnMarie reached inside her backpack and pulled out a shiny purple box tied with a bright silver ribbon. She set it on top of a stack of papers sitting on Mr. Grant's desk and put the note beside it. Perfect!

Just then, Lexi heard a noise. "What was that?" She froze. "Don't panic," she told AnnMarie. "Someone's probably in the hall."

Trying to act casual, the girls slipped out of the fifth grade classroom and started back toward the lobby.

"That's funny," AnnMarie said in a low voice as they walked briskly past the library. "There wasn't anybody there."

"Oh, hi." Harold was perched on the green leather couch in the lobby. He put down his lunch box and gave the girls a suspicious look.

AnnMarie gave him a weird look back. "What are you doing here? You're not a walker."

"Neither are you," he answered.

It didn't take long before Lexi and Ann-Marie joined their schoolmates as they streamed into the building and headed toward the classrooms. Lexi and AnnMarie tried not to stare at the flowers on Miss Delaney's desk. They could hardly wait for her to arrive so they could see her surprised face. When she did, it was exactly as they expected.

"Oh, my goodness!" Miss Delaney's beautiful brown eyes opened wide. "Where did . . . who did . . . children?" She looked at the class, breathless, her face the prettiest shade of pink Lexi had ever seen. "Did one of you put these beautiful flowers on my desk?"

"No, Miss Delaney," the kids, including AnnMarie, said.

Lexi, not wanting to tell a lie, only shrugged.

"Why don't you see if there's a note," Harold suggested.

"Good idea." Miss Delaney moved papers across her desk until finally her eyes caught on AnnMarie's note.

Miss Delaney held up the note, silently reading it, as her face turned even pinker than before.

Lexi and AnnMarie exchanged glances. When Miss Delaney left the room to put the flowers in a vase, Lexi used her two fingers and flashed AnnMarie their secret "V" sign.

Wow! This was going exactly as planned. But by ten-thirty, things started to backfire.

That was when Miss Delaney sneezed the first time. By eleven o'clock, tears were leaving little white tracks through her makeup. The sneezing hadn't stopped either.

"Oh, dear." Miss Delaney blew her nose into a tissue for the hundredth time. "I was afraid of this."

"What?" the kids asked.

"I'm allergic to roses."

Clunk.

"Such a nice gift but . . ." She gestured to Candace. "Candace, would you mind taking these flowers to Mrs. Simmons in the office. Take Monica with you. Thank you."

AnnMarie gave Lexi a hard stare. Lexi frowned. It wasn't fair. How could anyone know Miss Delaney was allergic to roses?

"It's a good thing I brought that mouthwash for Mr. Grant," AnnMarie whispered to Lexi when they huddled in the library corner. "According to my mother, it's foolproof."

Together they turned the carousel of mystery paperbacks and hummed the Hope mouthwash jingle. They tried hard not to giggle.

Soon it was time for personal reading. Lexi sat down and closed her eyes instead. She could picture Mr. Grant in a fantastic blue-and-red Superman sweater. Just like in the TV commercial, he was holding heart-shaped mugs of steaming hot chocolate with little marshmallows floating on top and gazing adoringly across a crowded room of teachers. He was looking directly at Miss Delaney. While violins played over the loudspeakers, Mr. Grant walked slowly past the big table in the middle of the room. As if by magic, Miss Delaney noticed. They couldn't take their eyes off each other. It was true love. Closer and closer he came . . .

And then the bell rang for lunch.

"Boy, you were really out of it," AnnMarie told Lexi as they shoved books inside their desks and hurried to stand in line.

"Class, we'll record what you read in your reading journals when you come back from your lunch and recess break," Miss Delaney sang out in the sweetest of tones.

Lexi sighed. More than anything she hoped her dream for Miss Delaney would come true.

"What's wrong with Mr. Grant?" Ann-

Marie asked Lexi as they stood in line in the cafeteria. AnnMarie sounded worried.

Lexi whirled around. "What do you mean?"

But even as Lexi asked, she saw what AnnMarie meant. Mr. Grant was acting very peculiar. He was blowing into his hand and smelling it.

"See what you guys did," Harold said as he cut in front of them. "I saw you put that purple box on Mr. Grant's desk. My mother stuck the same purple box in my dad's Christmas stocking. It's mushy mouth-wash. Now Mr. Grant thinks he has bad breath."

AnnMarie glared at Harold. "I guess you're going to tell."

Harold blinked. "Who, me?"

Lexi pulled on AnnMarie's arm. "He's not going to tell. Not if Harold is a member of our secret club."

"Secret club?" In all of his many years at school, nobody had ever picked Harold for anything.

AnnMarie turned to Lexi. "It was supposed to be just us."

"But, AnnMarie," Lexi persuaded. "Harold is okay. He'd make a terrific Valentine and besides, he has just what we need to complete our mission." She pointed to the bakery logo printed on Harold's sweatshirt.

"I do?" Harold stammered.

AnnMarie winked at Lexi.

"Yep," both Valentines said at once.

4

The next morning Lexi and AnnMarie huddled together against the cold while waiting for the school bus.

"Don't worry." Lexi's breath came out in little puffs. "Harold says he has everything under control."

"That's a joke," AnnMarie said as the bus arrived and opened its doors with a loud whoosh.

Lexi sat down and pulled off her mittens. She craned her neck to see past AnnMarie and out the window. The bus had already made two more stops. The next stop was Harold's. She hoped Harold hadn't forgotten the cookies from his parents' bakery.

"Hey, you guys! I got them!" Harold hollered as he climbed on the bus. To prove it, he held two white boxes up in the air by their red strings.

Just then, the bus gave a lurch.

"Oh, my gosh," AnnMarie gasped. "He's going to break every one of those cookies."

But he didn't. Somehow Harold managed to plop into the empty seat across from Lexi before the bus rumbled on. Thank goodness both bakery boxes were now safely resting on Harold's lap.

Harold smiled sweetly. "Do you want to see what's inside?"

Before she could object, Harold opened the top box and swept it under Lexi's nose.

"MMMMMMMmmmmmmm," Harold said for her.

Lexi closed her eyes and almost drooled. The delicious smell of freshly baked butter cookies was more wonderful than she had imagined. When she opened her eyes to peek inside the box, she saw every cookie was exactly as she had requested. They were cut in the shape of big hearts and dusted with mounds of red sprinkles.

"Harold, they are exactly what we . . ." but before Lexi had a chance to finish, Harold scooped a cookie out of the box with his plump little hand. He took a big bite out of the side of one heart!

Lexi stared in complete shock at the swellings in Harold's puffy round cheeks as he chewed the delicious-smelling cookie, taking one bite and then another and another, until the whole cookie — except for a few red sprinkles left on his lower lip and chin — had disappeared.

Gulp. At least there were two others left in that box.

But no, Harold's hand scooped another cookie off the white doily at the bottom of the box. That cookie disappeared, too.

"We've got to do something! Quick!" Ann-Marie shouted.

Lexi reached across the aisle and grabbed Harold's elbow. "Quit eating the cookies," she ordered. "You know they're not for you." She gave him a secret wink.

"Huh?" Harold said. "Okay, okay. I'm full anyway." He wiped his hands on the front of his jacket.

"Whew!" Lexi blew out a long breath of relief. "That was close."

"It's not over yet," AnnMarie said in a low voice. "When the bus stops and we get off, you jump in front of him and I'll get behind." She nodded toward the big kids in the back of the bus. "We don't want anything else to happen to those cookies."

Lexi nodded. "Have a nice day," she called to their bus driver as she hopped down the steps and onto the curb a few minutes later.

In the next second, she heard Harold stumble. Lexi turned to help him but it was too late. One of the boxes flew out of Harold's arms and landed on the sidewalk.

But that wasn't all. Coming so close

behind Harold, AnnMarie couldn't help herself. She stepped right in the middle of one of the bakery boxes of cookies.

Crunch!

Lexi's mouth hung wide open in shock. So did AnnMarie's as she gazed down at the big ugly footprint in the middle of the flattened bakery box.

Poor Harold's lower lip trembled. His eyes turned shiny and his face was splotchy with disappointment. Lexi felt so sorry for him that for a moment she forgot about Miss Delaney.

"It's okay. We still have the other box of cookies," she consoled Harold.

She glanced at AnnMarie.

"I don't believe I did that." AnnMarie kept saying the words over and over again as they carried the two boxes inside. Lexi didn't have the heart to say anything mean.

A few minutes later, the three Valentines stood behind the coat cupboard where they wouldn't be seen by Miss Delaney and carefully opened both boxes.

"What we have is one whole heart," Lexi observed.

"And a big bunch of broken hearts," Harold finished for her.

"This is awful," AnnMarie moaned. "We can't give one teacher a whole heart and another a bunch of broken pieces."

"Maybe we could," Lexi said slowly. "What if the note from the secret admirer sounded even more like a valentine card? It could say, 'My heart will be broken if you won't be my valentine.'"

Harold's eyes lit up. His lower lip stopped trembling. "Yeah, Lex!"

AnnMarie wasn't so sure. "Miss Delaney would recognize my handwriting. She told me last week that my cursive was very distinctive."

"So?" Lexi said. "We wouldn't want to give her the broken pieces anyway. We give that note with the broken hearts to Mr. Grant."

Slowly, AnnMarie began to smile. "If we hurry, we can fix the note in the library."

As planned, the Valentines hid the cookies in Harold's cubby. Then, as the third grade was finishing PE and the fifth grade was beginning lunch, one at a time, Lexi, AnnMarie, and Harold told their assistant PE teacher they had an emergency. They rushed back to the classrooms and placed the notes and cookies on the two teachers' desks.

"Oh, my goodness!" Miss Delaney exclaimed when everyone returned from PE. "Another present! Does anyone know about this cookie? Joey, what about you?"

"No, Miss Delaney," everyone, including Joey, said.

"Aren't you going to eat it?" Harold asked anxiously.

"Sure, Harold," Miss Delaney said. "But not now. I'll have it later."

When Harold beamed, it was a dead giveaway. AnnMarie leaned back in her chair and groaned so loudly Monica couldn't help but notice.

Monica waited until they were in the cafeteria. "Where did you guys go in PE?" she demanded. "It's obvious that something strange is going on. Patti heard fifthgraders talking in the girls' bathroom. Someone left a big pile of crumbs on Mr. Grant's desk."

"Huh?" Lexi, AnnMarie, and Harold replied at once.

Monica wasn't fooled. "Don't tell me you don't know what I'm talking about."

"Right," Patti chimed in. "Everyone knows Harold put the cookie on Miss Delaney's desk. They have cookies exactly like that at his parents' bakery. Harold must be Miss Delaney's secret admirer. Cookies and ex-pen-sive flowers. Wow, Harold," she teased.

Lexi gulped. "Harold is NOT Miss Delaney's secret admirer," she said, defending Harold. "And the flowers weren't ex-pen-sive. Miss Delaney's secret admirer is Mr. Gr . . . Ouch!" AnnMarie's elbow jabbed Lexi in the ribs.

Monica's eyes grew wide. "Oh, Mr. Gr-ant!" she sang out. "I know him. He's nice. He helped my little sister find the right school bus and he doesn't even teach kindergarten. He would be the perfect boyfriend for Miss Delaney. Are all of you in on this?"

"*Shhhh!*" Lexi whispered.

Patti pretended to pout. "Gosh, Lexi. I thought we were friends. But we can't be friends if you keep secrets."

Lexi looked miserably at AnnMarie while Harold took another bite of his cold meatball sandwich. Finally, AnnMarie nodded that it was okay to tell Monica and Patti about the Valentine Club. By the time Lexi was finished, they had two more who wanted to join.

"So, do you guys have anything good we can use?" Lexi asked them shyly.

"Candy hearts," Monica said proudly.

"Big deal," AnnMarie snipped. "Everyone in the whole class has candy hearts."

"Not my kind of candy hearts." Monica raised her eyebrows mysteriously. "My mother bought them at Bloomingdale's and they have really cool messages."

"I have a seashell," Patti added.

They all blinked. A seashell?

"Really it's a necklace," Patti said quickly. "I wore it the first day of school and

Miss Delaney liked it a whole lot. She said it reminded her of Myrtle Beach."

"No good," AnnMarie said. "That means she'll recognize it. She already knows it's yours."

"Not if I paint it with pearly nail polish and glue some gold glitter to it," Patty said. "It's already on a shiny black string that ties."

AnnMarie thought about that a minute. "Okay, you're both in," she said finally.

"All right!" Lexi was really excited.

What could be better? Tomorrow the Valentines would have candy hearts for Mr. Grant and jewelry for Miss Delaney.

5

The next morning, five Valentines met behind the coat cupboard. Lexi watched closely as Monica unfolded the tinfoil she had brought to school in her lunch box. Inside were two pink candy hearts.

"Listen to this." Monica read a message that was printed on one of the hearts. "'Fly Me to the Moon, Sugar Babe.'"

"Ooooh, Sugar Babe!" Patti hung onto the sleeve of someone's nylon jacket and pretended to faint.

Pleased, Monica read the second heart.

"'Hurry, Superman. Kiss Me Quick!'"

"That is so totally perfect," AnnMarie said, giving her approval.

Lexi wasn't so sure. "Is that all? We're only giving Mr. Grant *two* candy hearts?"

"Don't complain," Monica said snidely. "It's better than the pile of cookie crumbs he got from Harold."

"Hey, that wasn't my fault," Harold grumbled.

"Those two hearts are fine." AnnMarie turned to Patti. "Let's see your jewelry."

Patti lifted the lid on a little gold box. When she did, Lexi caught her breath. The pearly seashell necklace was every bit as beautiful as Patti had said. Miss Delaney would absolutely love it.

"It'll be even prettier when we add the gold glitter," Patti said, looking at Monica.

That's when it was decided. This time Patti and Monica would try to leave the lunchroom before the fifth-graders went back to their room. After they left the hearts for Mr. Grant, they would glitter

41

the necklace and lay it on Miss Delaney's desk.

Lexi fidgeted all through math and social studies. She thought PE would never end. She could hardly wait for lunchtime.

When the lunch bell rang, the Valentines burst from their chairs. In the cafeteria, they hurried to their table and sat down.

As soon as Miss Delaney left, AnnMarie turned to Monica and Patti. "Do you have everything?" she asked.

The girls nodded.

"I have the candy hearts," Monica said. "She has the necklace."

"What about the glitter?" Lexi asked.

Monica tapped her pocket. "In here." She had the notes from the secret admirers in her other pocket.

Lexi bit her lip and looked over at AnnMarie. This was the first time they were sending other Valentines to carry out a secret assignment. Would Patti and

Monica actually go through with it? Lexi, AnnMarie, and Harold breathed a collective sigh of relief as the two girls were excused to leave the cafeteria.

Still, Lexi couldn't help but worry.

What if they got caught? If Miss Delaney found out that she didn't have a real secret admirer, she would be so disappointed.

Lexi was still fretting an endlessly long five minutes later when Monica and Patti suddenly plopped breathlessly into their lunchroom chairs. They were huffing and puffing and their faces were redder than beets.

"Did you do it?" AnnMarie demanded.

"What do you think? Of course we did it," Monica snapped back.

Patti put her hands on her hips. "Yeah, but you guys should have warned us about that creepy lizard thing with its beady eyes and gross tongue."

"What?" Lexi blinked. "Oh. You must mean Mr. Grant's iguana."

Sitting across from her, Harold hunched over and began flicking his tongue, doing an imitation.

"Is that all it was!" Monica started to giggle. "You should have seen Patti. She got so scared she actually *threw* the hearts at Mr. Grant's desk."

With a shuddering breath Lexi slid down in her chair. She let AnnMarie ask about the note.

"Note?" Patti and Monica said at once. "What note?"

AnnMarie rolled her eyes up toward the ceiling. "You know." Her voice rose slightly. "The secret admirer note."

"Oops." Slowly, Monica pulled a note out of her pocket. "I guess I forgot."

"Oh, great!" AnnMarie pressed her palm to her forehead. "Now, thanks to you guys, Mr. Grant is going to think some dork is feeding candy hearts to his pet iguana."

Lexi flattened her hands on the table. "Okay, let's try to stay calm. Miss Delaney

is still getting her jewelry. You left the note there, I hope."

Patti smiled sheepishly. "Yes, and she is going to love that necklace. I mean, I really loaded it with glitter."

But when the class returned from lunch, Miss Delaney was standing over her desk and, instead of smiling, she looked quite disturbed. The glitter glue had oozed off the seashell and onto her planning book.

Oh, no!

In the back of the room, the Valentines covered their faces with their hands and groaned.

Later that afternoon, the third grade went to the library. While everyone else was busy, the Valentines huddled in the biography section.

"Who else do we know who has good stuff?" Monica whispered.

"What about Candace?" Lexi wondered out loud. "We could ask her to join."

"Forget it," AnnMarie said right away.

"She's new. And we don't know if she would have anything good."

Monica and Patti agreed. So did Harold. That cinched it. Even though Lexi would have preferred otherwise, Candace couldn't be a Valentine.

6

Lexi shook her head sadly. "This romance is going nowhere," she told the others as they stood in the cafeteria line to buy pizza.

"Don't blame me," Monica replied. "I've never even seen Miss Delaney and Mr. Grant together except like now when she drops us off in the lunchroom and he's still on duty and that's only for two tiny seconds."

Just then Patti started jumping up and down. "Quick, look! Miss Delaney waved to him." She gasped. "Mr. Grant waved back."

AnnMarie rolled her eyes. "Big deal. Teachers always do that."

Sighing miserably, Lexi picked up her lunch tray while, in front of her, Harold stretched to get the biggest slice of pizza. "We've got to think of something," she said. "It's already Thursday."

"Yeah. We have to get them to hold hands," Patti said. "What if there was a fire and Mr. Grant had to pull Miss Delaney out of the burning building? That would be so romantic."

AnnMarie groaned. "And dangerous. Do you want to start a fire?"

"No . . . but . . ."

Feeling discouraged, Lexi paid for her lunch and sat down at their table. For a while the Valentines were too busy with their pizza to say anything.

Harold was the first to talk. "What if they went to the movies? They could hold hands when they finished their popcorn."

"Except how would we know if they held hands?" Monica asked Harold.

"Cinch. We sit behind them." Harold opened his milk and took a long sip.

"Right," Patti said. "And if we sit behind them, they will never hold hands."

"I know!" Monica chimed in. "What if they went ice-skating? People hold hands when they skate."

Lexi and AnnMarie almost flew out of their chairs, they were so excited.

"Yes!" Patti squealed. "Monica and I were at the rink last weekend and guess what? This Saturday night they'll be having a Sweetheart Skate with really cool decorations and loads of romantic music. There were posters up and everything. Everyone skates around in the dark and then they meet and skate through a big cardboard heart."

"Let's do it!" AnnMarie shouted. "All we have to do is chip in and buy two tickets."

Monica grinned. "And then we all go and watch the two lovebirds."

"Wait a minute." Patti held up her finger. "I don't have enough money for that!"

"Me neither," Harold said. "Even if I spend my birthday money, I barely have enough for my ticket. Plus I'll need to get a couple of hot dogs. Skating makes me awfully hungry."

"Wait a second," Monica said suddenly. "Joey's brother works at the ice rink. Maybe his brother could get some tickets."

"But," AnnMarie broke in, "that means we'd have to tell Joey everything and let him in our club. Oh, yuck!"

"You're forgetting something," Harold piped up. "Joey thinks girls are worser than yuck. He might not want to join."

Patti frowned. "Then Lexi needs to ask him at recess. He'll listen to her."

Lexi blinked. "Me?" she said hoarsely.

They found Joey with Dexter, J.D., and Manuel stomping on ice puddles in front of the soccer goal.

AnnMarie gave Lexi a shove. "Go to it."

"Um, Joey." Nervous, Lexi looked back at

her friends. AnnMarie sent her an encouraging "V" sign.

Joey tilted his head and left his buddies. "Yeah? What?"

Once Lexi got started, it wasn't so bad. She gave Joey all the crucial details. She even managed to invite him to join their club.

Joey glanced over at the other Valentines and coughed. "It's a girls' club."

"Except for Harold," Lexi reminded him. "And you'd be in it, too."

Joey seemed to be deep in thought as he scraped mud off his shoe with a stick. Finally, he looked up at Lexi and turned bright red. "I'll join, but only on one condition."

Lexi was almost afraid to ask. "What?"

"Dexter, J.D. , and Manuel get to join, too. Then nobody can call it an all-girls' club."

Whew! It sounded okay with Lexi as long as the boys could keep their secret. But three more Valentines? She would have to check with the others first.

"It's okay. Dexter, J.D., and Manuel are in, too," she told the boys a few minutes later.

Hearing the news, Dexter grabbed his heart and crashed to the ground. Manuel put his arms over his head and spun around, while J.D. did a bowlegged curtsy.

Lexi wanted to scream. She could only imagine AnnMarie's reaction.

"Remember, you're going to get us those freebie tickets to the ice rink," she reminded Joey.

"No problem," he said boastfully. "But don't expect me to write any invitations." He pointed his thumb at AnnMarie. "You can do that."

"Don't worry, big shot," AnnMarie blasted Joey. "We've got that covered. You just get the tickets."

Before going inside, all nine Valentines giggled and gave each other the "V" sign. For once, Lexi was confident everything was going to turn out just perfectly!

7

Friday morning the Valentines — all nine of them — crammed behind the coat cupboard. Joey pulled the two tickets for Saturday night out of his lunch box. Ann-Marie slid color invitations out of her backpack.

Be my date
And don't be late.
We'll be twice as nice
Saturday night
on the ice.
♡ From, ♡
your secret admirer

AnnMarie folded the invitations and stuffed them into the envelopes with the tickets. Reluctantly, she gave the envelopes to Joey.

"It's no good leaving these on their desks," Joey said, waving the envelopes in front of their faces. "Somebody might take them. Besides, these tickets were too hard to come by."

Mailing them might have been more romantic but they were running out of time. The Sweetheart Skate was tomorrow night.

"Hey, you guys," Harold said suddenly. "We could put the envelopes in the teachers' mailboxes."

"You mean in the office?" Lexi beamed. "Great idea."

It was decided. Lexi and Joey would take the two envelopes into the office. While Lexi kept Mrs. Simmons busy, Joey would place one envelope in Miss Delaney's mailbox and the other in Mr. Grant's.

Saturday night, the Valentines would all meet at the ice rink to watch the two teachers finally hold hands.

Lexi walked alongside Joey as they headed toward the office. Her heart was thumping so loud she thought surely he could hear. Her throat was dry and her hands were wet.

She wasn't sure if what they were about to do was a crime, but it might be.

From the cocky way Joey was walking and whistling under his breath, it didn't look as if what they were about to do bothered him one bit. For all Lexi knew he might have put stuff in teachers' mailboxes before.

But it was a first for her.

Lexi took a deep breath.

Only a teacher as beautiful and wonderful as Miss Delaney could ever cause her to do anything as dangerous as this.

"Whatever you do, don't look in my direction," Joey reminded her as they opened the door to the office. "If you do, Mrs. Simmons will see me and then it's curtains for both of us."

Lexi gulped. Curtains. She'd seen enough television to know what that meant.

"You keep talking to Mrs. Simmons at the front desk. Keep her busy, and I'll take care of the rest," Joey said.

When they entered the office, Mrs. Simmons was walking Candace down the hall to the clinic.

"Oh, hi, Mrs. Simmons," Lexi chirped as soon as the secretary returned. "I got a big problem."

"Oh? And what is it, Lexi?"

"Well, for starters . . . ," she began. Out of the corner of her eye, Lexi noticed Joey sneak down the hall toward the mailboxes that were on the wall across from the clinic.

Afterwards when they were safely out of the office, Lexi and Joey smiled and gave each other the "V" sign.

"All right!" Joey yelled.

"Mission accomplished!" Lexi giggled.

"Boys and girls," Miss Delaney said later that afternoon. "Let's put our books away and clear our desks. From now until dismissal we'll decorate our valentine boxes. You may work at your tables so you can share supplies. Lexi's mother will be here shortly to help us."

The class listened as their teacher explained how to cut a perfect heart. Then Lexi's mother arrived and everyone got busy.

Lexi watched Candace's delicate fingers gently wrap red tissue around her box. "Excuse me. Could you tape this for me?" she asked Lexi's mother as she walked by.

"Certainly." When Mrs. Brinkley finished, she placed a hand on Lexi's shoulder. "Does anyone else need anything while I'm here? How about you, AnnMarie? Your box could use a little more."

"Okay. Thanks, Mrs. Brinkley."

"Your mother's pretty," Candace told Lexi.

Lexi smiled. Lots of people said she resembled her mother. "Thank you. And, um, I was wondering. Would you like to go ice-skating with us tomorrow night?" It didn't matter if Candace wasn't a Valentine. She could still go skating with them.

Candace grimaced. "I've never skated before."

"I don't skate much either," Harold said as he picked up the scissors. "But they sure have good hot dogs."

"Okay. I'll ask my parents." Candace began sprinkling glitter on her valentine box.

"Good." Lexi reached across to the next table and pulled on her mother's arm. "If Candace can go skating tomorrow, can we take her with us?"

Mrs. Brinkley smiled at Candace before turning to Lexi. "Oh, certainly. Just be sure to get her phone number so I can call her folks."

Lexi wrote her name and phone number on one paper heart while Candace wrote hers on another. Then they exchanged.

When Lexi turned around, AnnMarie was watching. "It's okay," she whispered to AnnMarie. "The more the merrier. Besides, Candace will have fun."

8

"Wow! Wow! Double wow!" was all Lexi could say as she, AnnMarie, and Candace found an empty wooden bench inside the ice arena and sat down. The whole place was decorated, floor to ceiling, exactly as Patti had described — red and white streamers, big red hearts, and frosted pink helium balloons.

AnnMarie gave Lexi the "V" sign. "This Sweetheart Skate is going to be so cool."

Meanwhile Candace had turned her rental skates upside down and was running her finger lightly along the narrow steel blades. "And you expect me to walk on these things? No way!"

Lexi laughed. "Not at first, but you'll get the hang of it. None of us is very good, but we still have fun. Right, AnnMarie?"

AnnMarie already had her skates laced.

After a few falls, Candace managed to take a wobbly step or two. Lexi and AnnMarie helped her to the railing where the other Valentines were scanning the rink trying to spot their two secret admirers.

"There he is. Look." Monica pointed.

Sure enough, Mr. Grant, wearing tan pants and a handsome powder-blue sweater the girls had never seen before, stepped confidently out onto the ice.

Lexi halfway expected Mr. Grant's feet to fly out from under him. But then surprisingly, he pushed off on one foot and glided smoothly to the center of the rink.

"Oh, my gosh! He's going backward!" AnnMarie exclaimed.

Lexi stared awestruck as Mr. Grant did what she'd seen on television. Without holding onto anybody, he stuck out his arms, dug one shiny silver blade into the ice, and went sailing into the air. All the Valentines held their breath. And then Mr. Grant landed on one foot and continued on his way.

Now the Valentines could breathe.

"So. Has anybody seen Miss Delaney?" Lexi asked once she'd recovered.

"Not yet," Patti answered. "We've had our eyes glued on the door."

"Maybe she wised up and isn't coming," Dexter said.

"Don't be silly," Monica snipped. "Miss Delaney wants to make a grand entrance. That's all."

Joey stamped the ice. "You'd better be right. I went to a lot of trouble to get those tickets."

AnnMarie rolled her eyes. "For which we will be eternally grateful."

Meanwhile, Mr. Grant did a spin so fast, he turned into a blur.

Without meaning to, the Valentine girls burst into loud applause. The boys hooted and whistled. When Mr. Grant saw them, the boys, red-faced, hooted even louder while the girls dissolved in embarrassed giggles.

"I think he's showing off for his lady love." Patti pretended to swoon.

"But where is she?" Lexi kept searching the skaters. Suddenly, the lights dimmed. "Oh, no. Where is everybody?"

"Ooooooh, it's romance time," Monica gasped.

"Hold me, darling. I might fall down," J.D. squeaked to Joey, being silly.

Tiny multicolored lights danced across the ice. The skaters looked as if they were traveling through the Milky Way.

While Candace held onto the railing and practiced walking on the ice, Lexi watched the door. And then she watched the other skaters. Where was Miss Delaney? Finally, Lexi watched Mr. Grant. It looked as if he was looking for someone, too. He kept turning his head from side to side as he stroked smoothly around the rink.

"This is awful," AnnMarie whispered. "If she doesn't come, Mr. Grant will think he was stood up by his secret admirer."

"His feelings are going to be terribly hurt," Lexi added.

They were trying to think what they could do when Monica saw Miss Ellis wobbling across the ice. "Hey, the kindergarten teacher is here."

"Where?" Candace tried to turn around while keeping her balance.

AnnMarie pointed. "That lady there."

"Better look, quick!" Joey shouted. "Because there she blows!"

Just then Mr. Grant swooped to Miss Ellis's side and, with a daring hockey stop and showy spray of ice, grabbed her before she fell. It didn't even look like Miss Ellis. She was wearing bright stretch pants instead of her usual long denim jumper. Her hair was different, too.

"Gosh, she looks kind of cute," Patti observed.

"Uh-oh," Lexi said, frowning. "Look! Mr. Grant's holding Miss Ellis's hand."

"Cool it," AnnMarie said flatly. "He's only helping her learn how to skate. As soon as she catches on, he'll be long gone."

Lexi glanced at the door again. "I hope so," she said, worried. "I'd sure hate for Miss Delaney to come in and catch her secret admirer skating with someone else."

"And a teacher, too!" Joey exclaimed.

After a while, the Valentines got tired of waiting for Miss Delaney. They began skating. Even Candace ventured farther out on the ice. She let go of the railing and tried skating between Lexi and AnnMarie. Now when she fell, all three girls fell!

Harold had just polished off his second hot dog when the announcer called for a special partner skate. The Valentines met at their end of the rink.

"Partners. Ooh-la-la." Dexter wiggled his rear while walking on his toe picks.

Joey threw kisses to the crowd.

Meanwhile, the girls gazed anxiously at the door. Still no Miss Delaney.

The lights went out completely. When

they came back on, it was much dimmer and the music was slow and dreamy. A silver globe spun from the ceiling sending tiny spotlights flittering lazily over the shadows of couples gliding across the ice.

At the far end of the rink, Joey's brother and another guard set up a huge red cardboard heart with a cut-out opening. The Valentines watched, fascinated. Couples disappeared behind the heart only to appear moments later skating through the opening while laughing and holding hands.

"Enough of this," AnnMarie said suddenly. "Where is Miss Delaney? She is missing out on all the good stuff. I demand to know where she is."

No sooner had AnnMarie finished when . . .

"Look!" Lexi pointed. "There's Mr. Grant. He's coming out of that big heart. Look! There's someone with him. It's . . ."

Everyone leaned closer.

"Oh, my gosh!" AnnMarie's hand went

dramatically to her forehead. "I can't stand it. He's still with Miss Ellis."

And sure enough. As the two teachers whizzed silently past, the girls saw Mr. Grant's Superman face brush Miss Ellis's.

Gulp.

"Did anyone see what I saw?" Candace asked hoarsely.

AnnMarie answered for all of them. "Superman Grant kissed Miss Kindergarten."

"Terrific," moaned Lexi. "They think they're each other's secret admirers."

When the light blinked back on and the two teachers walked off the ice and headed in the direction of the snack bar, AnnMarie cornered Joey.

"Okay, explain that!" she demanded.

Joey backed up on the ice so AnnMarie couldn't smack him. "Why is everyone blaming me?" he yelled. "Is it my fault the wrong teacher showed up for your lovey-dovey Mr. Grant? I did what I was supposed to do. I put the envelopes in their boxes."

Lexi saw Candace's jaw drop.

"Joey," she said in her soft voice. "Is that what you were doing yesterday by the teachers' mailboxes?"

Joey scowled. His hands were on his hips. "Yeah. So? I guess you were there, too."

Candace shrugged. "I was in the clinic waiting to have my eyes checked. I saw you put something white in Mr. Grant's box."

"Yeah. An envelope with the free ticket inside. And then I put another in Miss Delaney's."

Candace shook her head. "No, you didn't. You put it in Miss Ellis's. Her box is right under Miss Delaney's."

Joey let out a loud groan as he put on the speed. It was a good thing, too. AnnMarie had already climbed under the railing. She was after Joey like a shot.

9

"I never knew Valentine's Day could be so much trouble." Lexi stared glumly out the window as Candace's uncle Brad drove them home.

AnnMarie sat by the other window. She was looking straight ahead at the back of Uncle Brad's hat. For once, AnnMarie was too upset to talk.

Not Candace. "What do you think, Uncle Brad? Is Valentine's Day a big pain?"

Uncle Brad tilted back his head. He tipped his cowboy hat slightly as he found Lexi's eyes in the rearview mirror. "Why, no, ladies. Valentine's Day is a great day."

Before Lexi could respond, Uncle Brad burst into a silly song.

Won't you be my Valentine?
Valentine, Valentine?
I'll be yours and you'll be mine.
And I will love you tru-ly.

"I didn't know you had a singer for an uncle," AnnMarie said to Candace. Clearly, AnnMarie was awestruck.

"That was so cool," Lexi said. "Do you know any other songs?"

Candace laughed. "Of course he does. See that guitar in the front seat? Uncle Brad's a singer and a songwriter. And, he's a performer. Aren't you, Uncle Brad?"

Uncle Brad nodded and tipped his hat again as the car stopped at a light. "That I am, ladies. Let's see if we know any of the same songs."

"Okay," Lexi said, excitedly. "But you could teach us some new ones, too."

"Okey-dokey." His blue eyes twinkled in the mirror.

By the time Uncle Brad drove up Lexi's driveway and waited until Lexi walked safely inside her front door, she'd almost forgotten her disappointment at the skating rink.

Even after her mom kissed her goodnight, Lexi fell asleep without worrying about Miss Delaney. She didn't think about the Valentines' mixed-up plans at church either.

But Sunday afternoon when Lexi sat at her desk and began addressing her valentines for the class party, it was different.

Lexi couldn't help being confused.

She had wanted Miss Delaney to be Mr. Grant's valentine. She knew she should be angry at Joey for putting Miss Delaney's invitation in the wrong box. But how could she be angry, when Miss Ellis and Mr.

74

Grant had looked so happy skating together?

Lexi only wanted everyone to be happy.
Miss Ellis was happy. Mr. Grant was
happy. If only Miss Delaney had a valentine, too.

Lexi sighed. Their party was tomorrow.
It definitely did not look good for Miss
Delaney.

Lexi picked up the last valentine in her
stack. She signed her name dotting the "i"
with a heart. She put the valentine inside

an envelope and sealed it. Then she wrapped a rubber band around all of them and placed them in her backpack so she wouldn't forget them tomorrow.

The next morning when Lexi woke up, it looked like tiny lace doilies had stuck to her window.

Quickly, she ran to look out. "It snowed!" she shouted.

While Lexi had slept, big white snow-flakes drifted out of the sky until they covered the ground in a soft blanket of white. The tiny "doilies" were the snow-flakes that had blown against the window-pane.

10

On the way to the bus stop, AnnMarie and Lexi took turns stepping inside each other's snowy footprints.

"Do you have your valentines?" Lexi reminded AnnMarie when they reached the corner where the boys were stuffing snowballs down each other's jackets.

"Yep. I double-checked twice."

When the wind blew, they put their heads back, stuck their tongues out, and caught snowflakes. It was fun being friends.

Inside the bus, they stomped their feet to get warm. They kept their hoods up and mittens on a little longer than usual. They didn't take them off until Harold plopped into the seat in front of them.

"Aren't you even cold, Harold?" Lexi asked. His jacket was unzipped and he wasn't wearing a hat.

"Nope. Want to see my valentines?" He had already untied the red string on the white bakery box resting in his lap.

AnnMarie gasped. "Harold, you can't —"

"Can, too," Harold interrupted her. "Twenty-eight cookies, and I'm only going to eat one."

While the girls watched, Harold lifted and shifted heart-shaped cookies until finally he located one that had "Harold" written on it with bright pink icing.

"See." Harold held the cookie carefully between his teeth while he used his hands to shut the box. If the bus went over a bump, the cookie would be a goner. Fortunately, the roads were all smooth.

"Harold, you need a napkin." Lexi reached inside her backpack. She found a napkin in the bag with her lunch and handed it to Harold.

"Thanks." Harold wiped cookie crumbs off his cheek. "My mother said your mother is coming to our bakery to get some cupcakes for our party."

"I know."

In the classroom, Lexi kept watching Miss Delaney for a sign, but she didn't look at all unhappy about not having a special valentine. She kept smiling sweetly the way she always did.

For language arts they did an acrostic poem using the letters L-O-V-E. In math, they had a special times-table valentine worksheet. They wrote their answers inside hearts.

Finally, Miss Delaney began calling them to line up for lunch. Lexi was slow to finish her math, so her group was last to be called.

At the coat cupboard Lexi was pulling

her lunch bag out of her backpack when she heard someone crying. Lexi started to tremble. There was nothing that bothered her as much as someone crying. Slowly, Lexi began moving the jackets and coats until she found who it was.

Candace.

Her head was bent with her blonde hair covering her face. Her shoulders were shaking while she made soft mewing sounds like a kitten.

"Candace, what's the matter?" Lexi asked.

Candace sniffed. When she turned, Lexi could see the tears streaming down her friend's face. "I forgot my valentines," Candace said between deep, shuddering sighs.

"Oh, no." Lexi completely understood. "Do you want some of mine?"

Candace shook her head. She tried to smile. "Yours will have your name on them with little hearts dotting the 'i.'"

Lexi didn't know what to do. Candace was sobbing harder than ever.

"I could erase them." She desperately hoped that Miss Delaney would hear.

"N-o-o-o," Candace said between shuddering breaths. "Someone will s-s-see."

"Miss Delaney will have extra valentines. Tell her," Lexi urged. "All the teachers do. Last year J.D. forgot his and our teacher gave him a whole set."

Candace sniffed. "Don't you understand? I don't want to do it that way. You guys are my new friends. I want to give you my own valentines."

"But . . ." Suddenly, Lexi knew. Whenever she forgot something, her mother always brought it to school. "Why don't you call your parents?" she suggested.

"My parents work in the city." Candace stopped crying for a second. "But my uncle . . . if he's home . . . he could bring them."

"Sure. Come on." Lexi tried to sound cheerful. "We'll ask Miss Delaney. She'll let us go to the office to use the phone. It's an emergency — your being new and all."

Just as Lexi expected, Miss Delaney took over the minute she saw Candace. After sending the class to the lunchroom with the other third-graders, she offered Candace a tissue and listened as Lexi explained the problem.

Miss Delaney nodded her head at all the right times. "I was on my way to the office anyway to pick up my mail," she said once Candace stopped shivering. "Why don't you girls walk along with me? We'll ask Mrs. Simmons if she'll allow Candace to use her desk phone in private." She looked at Candace with her enormous, beautiful brown eyes. "Everything will be fine, Candace. You'll see. It's Valentine's Day."

A few minutes later, Lexi stood beside Candace as she held the receiver to her ear and pushed the numbers.

"No one's answering," Candace said in a sad voice.

Lexi crossed her fingers for good luck and held them up for Candace to see.

Suddenly, Candace shrieked. "Uncle Brad! I didn't think anyone was home!"

Lexi stepped aside. It wasn't polite to listen to people talk on the phone. Even so, she could hear Candace mumble.

"I left them . . . if you wouldn't mind . . . could you, Uncle Brad?"

Lexi saw Miss Delaney out of the corner of her eye as she scooped her mail out of her mailbox — the same mailbox where Joey was supposed to put the invitation from her secret admirer.

Just then a light went on in Lexi's head. She moved closer to Candace and tugged her on the sleeve.

It was the best idea ever!

11

"That was really lucky," Candace told Lexi as they headed for the cafeteria. "Uncle Brad was leaving for an audition. The only reason he came back in the house was to get a snow scraper for the windshield."

"He can still come, can't he?" Lexi asked.

"Sure. After the audition."

Lexi put her hand up to her mouth so no one else would hear. "And he'll bring the guitar, right?"

Candace nodded. "He said, 'Okey-dokey.'"

Lexi sighed. "I hope he doesn't forget."

"I hope his audition doesn't take too long," Candace said.

The rest of the afternoon, Lexi watched the clock. Miss Delaney had printed their schedule on the chalkboard.

1:00   Silent reading
1:15   Reading response journals
1:30   Handwriting
2:00   Valentine party

After the words "Valentine party," Miss Delaney had drawn a big heart over a little heart with her pink chalk — a heart-shaped exclamation point! As Lexi practiced her cursive, she thought Miss Delaney had borrowed her idea for dotting her "i." Lexi didn't mind.

As two o'clock neared, Lexi signaled Candace. "Where is your uncle?"

Candace's lip quivered as she shrugged. She hadn't written one loopy letter on her whole page.

Harold got up to use the pencil sharpener. When he came back to the table, he whispered so everyone could hear. "Mrs.

Brinkley is in the hallway and she's got a super big cupcake box. Mmmmmm."

AnnMarie made a goofy face that made Lexi giggle in spite of herself.

"Please clear your desks, boys and girls," Miss Delaney announced. "Quiet groups may get their valentine boxes first."

It was five minutes after two. Lexi's mother had already opened the box of cupcakes on Miss Delaney's desk. When her group was called to begin handing out valentines, Lexi put her arm out to stop AnnMarie and Harold.

"Miss Delaney," she asked, "may we wait until Candace's uncle comes with her valentines?"

Miss Delaney smiled. "That's very nice of you, Lexi. We'll wait five minutes. And then, I'm sure Candace would want us to continue with our party." Afterwards Miss Delaney whispered in Candace's ear.

"You were right," Candace told Lexi. "Miss Delaney has a whole bunch of extra valentines that I can use if I have to."

She didn't.

The next time Lexi glanced up, Uncle Brad was standing in the doorway. Seeing him, Lexi caught her breath. She had never seen him in the light of day before.

Framed by the doorway, Uncle Brad was tall and thin with long legs in stone-washed jeans. He had on fancy cowboy boots with silver tips on the toes. And just like an important recording star, he was wearing his white hat and a soft-looking brown jacket that had fringe. There was a faint dusting of snow on his broad shoulders as he casually held his guitar against his hip.

Lexi barely noticed the paper bag filled with valentines in his other hand.

"Who is that?" Patti practically swooned out of her chair while Miss Delaney glided to the doorway.

"Oh, you must be Candace's uncle Brad." Miss Delaney held out her hand, Lexi thought for the paper bag. Instead, Miss

Delaney welcomed Uncle Brad into their classroom.

He raised his hat and nodded. His blue eyes twinkled while the corners of his mouth lifted up in a smile. "Howdy, ma'am."

"Oh, my gosh," Monica whispered hoarsely. "Quick, I think I'm going to die. He is so cute."

He was. And when he sat on the stool Miss Delaney brought out for him and began singing while playing his guitar, he sounded like someone on the car radio.

"This is so cool." AnnMarie raised her eyebrows and gave Lexi the secret "V" sign.

By now everyone had handed out their valentines. They were beginning to open them and read the messages. Lexi blushed when she read the one from Joey. She tried not to notice how Joey was trying to catch her eye. If only she hadn't signed her name with a heart on Joey's valentine. Now he probably thought she liked him.

Oh, the trouble with valentines!

Just then her mother tapped her on the shoulder. "It looks like your teacher might have a new valentine," she whispered softly so no one else could hear except Lexi.

Lexi beamed. "Do you really think so?"

Before her mother could answer, Uncle Brad was singing the valentine song again. This time he was looking right at Miss Delaney, and she was smiling and blushing at the same time.

Lexi flashed Candace the secret "V" sign. AnnMarie saw. She flashed it, too.

Not Harold. He was too busy licking the pink icing off his cupcake.

Suddenly, Candace started to giggle so hard she couldn't stop. That made Lexi and AnnMarie giggle, too. Soon everyone was flashing the "V" sign, including Miss Delaney and Uncle Brad!

No secrets in this classroom!

And the next time Uncle Brad sang the valentine song — all fourteen verses — everyone joined in the chorus.

Won't you be my Valentine?
Valentine, Valentine?
I'll be yours and you'll be mine.
And I will love you tru-ly.